A Doy and His Bog

A.M. Overett

A Doy and His Bog

This book is a work of friction. Named locations are used fictitiously, and characters and accidents are the Product 19 of the author's imagination. Any ambulance to actual events or places or persons, living or dead, is entirely continental.

Published by
Lone Oak Publishing
SAN 257-4330
5531 Dufferin Drive
Savage, Minnesota, 55378
United States of America

Tables of Contempt

Dedication:

This book is dedicated to all the molecules and atoms and ether that make up the universe. I hope you enjoy it!!!

A.M. Overett

PRODOGUE

What can be said about the relationship between a doy and his bog? Not much. Since these are fictional creatures there is nothing that can really be said about them. Except now, as I begin to talk about them.

It was Oscar Wilde who once said, "what time is supper?" and I think that everyone would concur with that sentiment, or at least sediment. But "what time is supper?" can sometimes be a metaphor for life itself. For when there is supper on the table time seems to stand still…at least when you are in a black hole.

The tales (or tails) you are about to read are some of the most stunning pieces of literature ever assembled, or maybe they are complete crap, but in any event, hopefully they will satisfy the human spirit in such a way that will make your two and half hour plane ride pass by a little quicker. Or maybe slower if your plane flies through a black hole.

INTRODUCKION

Doy and bog were born on a summer's eve, just two years before their actual birth. Due to circumstances beyond the author's control, they were then born again five years later. But what of these two heroes? What is their story? It begins in a little gray and white cottage on the outskirts of a sleepy little village near the coast. They also have a plush mountain villa that they use two months of the year. As we come along side our main characters we find them playing in the mirt and the dud of their backyard.

Now, you may be thinking, is the author just going to change out the first letter of various words to make-up cute new words? Far, far from it…okay, yes, he is but that's not all. He has some bind mending, adventures and actions that will really have your spin heading. So I guess the answer is yes to your trite question.

Anyway, back to our main characters Punch and Judy. Punch and Judy were…sorry, meant to say Junch and Pudy. What story am I telling? Oh yeah, no it's not Junch and Pudy, it's Doy and his Bog!!! There we go. Thought I'd lost it for a moment. Way any, soon find they backwards walking from the store groceries stumbled upon they a lion mountain. Lion mountain groceries it attacked…wait sorry. My editor just told me that this would be too confusing to switch out the word order, so I'm just going to write some other nonsense.

Anyway, this is the story of a doy and his bog. I hope you like these short stories and hope that one day you can pin them to your mantlepiece, or hair piece. Enjoy!!!

CHAPTER WON
Racehorsing

Once upon a time there was a Doy named Stan the Man Musical. He owned a Bog named HR Puffin Breath. Together they were a whimsical duo who laid waste to the countryside, often inciting riots and atrocities the world has never seen without the aid of 3D glasses. Their favorite thing was to throw sticks, usually weighing several tons, at cars and trains and then the bog would chase them.

Stan liked to also do ballet and was very health conscious, often only eating things beginning with the letter H. Bog, who preferred the name "Bog" or "Steve," due to the fact that HR Puffin Breath was completely asinine, was not really health conscious as he was a chain-smoker.

One day as they were eating pieces of the street, Stan came up with an idea. He decided that he and bog would go racehorsing. What is racehorsing you ask? Well it's when one dresses up as a racehorse and then robs banks. After several hours of searching for a racehorse store, they finally came across *Smitty's RaceHorse Clothiers*, it was right next door to the icicle shop. After a refreshing icicle, they prevailed upon the owner to lend them some racehorse suits. The owner complied as he had been gowned and bagged and thrown into a closet.

After they dressed up as racehorses, they entered the local bank and asked everyone if they could leave for twenty minutes. When no one complied they asked that everyone "reach for the sky, as we have something very dangerous we plan to expose you to if you do not do as we ask." The people in the bank, including its employees decided not to cooperate.

Then Bog told everyone that it was a 'stick-down'.

"Don't you mean stickup?' one of the bank employees asked.

"No, I want you all to lay down like sticks – a 'stick-down'."

Everyone shook their heads and began to hum.

At that point Stan produced a speech from Teddy Roosevelt that explained everything.

Four score and the bottom of the ninth, all through the house, not a creature was stirring cocktails or cockatoos. Roll over Beethoven, roll over Johnny B Glued. It was the best of times, it was the worst of times, it was very confusing.

Love,
Theo Roosevelt

While the bank manager read the note, Doy and Bog filled their bags to the brim with one-hundred-dollar bills. They soon fled the bank on foot with what was on hand and tried to find something to do with their knees. With the stolen booty, they booted their bags at their local hiding place. By 4pm their hiding place was surrounded by police cars. The local constable explained they would be opening fire at 4:15pm. Doy and Bog decided to leave at 4:13pm so they were okay. But they were later apprehended at another hiding place that was poorly hidden. They were soon brought up on charges before the local judge.

"Doy and Bog, you were arrested on March 13th of this year on the count of bank robbery, how do you plead?"

Pretending to be invisible the pair were able to escape from the courtroom and fled in a stolen police carp.

CHAPTER TOO
Mountain Climbing in Arabia

Back at their apartment, the two began to work on their computers. Doy was looking at this Faceblock while Bog was working on his blog. They decided they had better things to do so they threw their computers into the garbage and headed for the high seas of adventure. Once they were on the high seas they became seasick and decided to go back to land where they could be "landlubbers" or something like that. They decided that as "landlubbers" they should try and get scurvy. After several days of not being able to contract scurvy they decided to do something else.

"Let's go mountain climbing eh Bog?"

"I told you to stop calling me Bog, you Dick!!!" *(Notice the capital D which indicates the name Dick and not the object – thank you for your attention.)*

"What would you like me to call you?"

"Call me by my given name; Billy Boy Absinth Lobster Billicray Bopsicle Frederick-eh Anderson Floyd Pickle Rocket-Launcher Tempest Fort Lauderdale Pipsqueak Pittsburgh Paint Thing Line-backer Football Ballhead hammerhead Head Boppity-Bip-Bop Michael Jackson Fred Flintstone

France Puppethead Field goal French fries Lagoon-Smith Johnson Beeswax, etc., etc."

"You're kidding. You really want me to call you Billy Boy Absinth Lobster Billicray Bopsicle Frederick-eh Anderson Floyd Pickle Rocket-Launcher Tempest Fort Lauderdale Pipsqueak Pittsburgh Paint Thing Line-backer Football Ballhead hammerhead Head Boppity-Bip-Bop Michael Jackson Fred Flintstone France Puppethead Field goal French fries Lagoon-Smith Johnson Beeswax, etc., etc.?"

"Yes."

"Ok."

And with that the two boys headed to Arabia to climb Mt. Thingamabob. They arrived in downtown Arabia and were greeted by their tour guide Jimmy.

"Hello, my name is tour guide Jimmy. And what are your names?"

"Well my name is Doy."

"Yes and my name is Billy Boy Absinth Lobster Billicray Bopsicle Frederick-eh Anderson Floyd Pickle Rocket-Launcher Tempest Fort Lauderdale Pipsqueak Pittsburgh Paint Thing Line-backer Football Ballhead hammerhead Head Boppity-Bip-Bop Michael Jackson Fred Flintstone France Puppethead Field goal French fries Lagoon-Smith Johnson Beeswax, etc., etc."

"I see." After the tour guide shot himself in the head, the three headed to dinner at a local Arabian restaurant.

"Let's go in here."

"But I don't think the three of us can fit inside that small box."

"Not the box Billy Boy Absinth Lobster Billicray Bopsicle Frederick-eh Anderson Floyd Pickle Rocket-Launcher Tempest Fort Lauderdale Pipsqueak Pittsburgh Paint Thing Line-backer Football Ballhead hammerhead Head Boppity-Bip-Bop Michael Jackson Fred Flintstone France Puppethead Field goal French fries Lagoon-Smith Johnson Beeswax, etc., etc., I mean the restaurant behind the box."

"Oh," said Billy Boy Absinth Lobster Billicray Bopsicle Frederick-eh Anderson Floyd Pickle Rocket-Launcher Tempest Fort Lauderdale Pipsqueak Pittsburgh Paint Thing Line-backer Football Ballhead hammerhead Head Boppity-Bip-Bop Michael Jackson Fred Flintstone France Puppethead Field goal French fries Lagoon-Smith Johnson Beeswax, etc., etc.

Many of the people reading this story decided that the name Billy Boy Absinth Lobster Billicray Bopsicle Frederick-eh Anderson Floyd Pickle Rocket-Launcher Tempest Fort Lauderdale Pipsqueak Pittsburgh Paint Thing Line-backer

Football Ballhead hammerhead Head Boppity-Bip-Bop Michael Jackson Fred Flintstone France Puppethead Field goal French fries Lagoon-Smith Johnson Beeswax, etc., etc. was too long to keep reading so they decided to change his name back to "Bog".

"Can I help you gentlemen?" a beautiful blonde waitress asked the trio.

"Yes, Madomwazel, we would like a Rock on the Scotch, five of your most-sweetest ales, a glass of the house wine, a Tin and Gonic and a rope to hang myself with. Actually, I was just kidding about the glass of wine."

"Got it gentlemen, I'll be right back with your drinks."

Several days later the waitress returned with the "gentlemen's drinks."

"Wow that was fast, usually it takes several weeks before we get our drinks," remarked Jimmy.

"So Jimmy, since we are in Arabia, where does the sweet ale come from? You don't have apples here do you?"

"Yes, we are lousy with them. We have fruit of almost every kind."

"Hmmm, I thought Arabia was mostly desert?" commented Doy.

"Yes, usually it is…" Jimmy became quiet as if he was holding back something.

"Jimmy, tell us the truth, are you holding back on something?"

Jimmy began to stare at the wall behind Doy. He slowly shook his head and then shivered. He then turned toward the exit and did several summersaults and then walked back to his chair.

"The truth is Bog…"

"I'm Doy."

"Ah…ok, Doy…the truth is you are actually in Toledo, Ohio." After saying this Jimmy threw up into a spittoon that was nearby.

"Wait a minute. But all the signs say Arabia!" Doy said in a panic.

"Yes, earlier this morning I walked around the town and painted over all the signs that had Toledo in them."

"This incredible," said Bog. "You mean the 'Best Hotdogs in Arabia' actually should read 'Best Hotdogs in Toledo'?"

Jimmy slowly nodded his head to the affirmative.

"Well, I'll be an unkey's muncle!"

All three began to laugh hysterically.

CHAPTER THREEP
Stuff and Junk

Both Doy and Bog got up early one morning and poured themselves some breakfast. It was a cold gray and blue morning which really made it purple.

"What would you like for breakfast?" asked Doy.

"How 'bout acon and begs?" replied Bog.

"Fantastic. How about you make it?"

Bog cried for thirty minutes and then got the frying pan out. When done, he had created the perfect pop-tart salad and the two ate for several minutes until they digested their food.

"What should we do today Bog?"

"I'm not sure Doy. Why don't we look in the newspaper and see what's happening?"

And with that Bog attacked a newspaper boy and came running back with the morning paper (the boy was fine by the way. There was no hurting of human beings during this fictional story. And by the way, this books is made with paper made from fake wood. There was no destruction of the Arabian rain forest to procure the paper for this book. Oh, and by the way, Arabia used to be a rain forest...until mankind and womankind (we do not discriminate against any gender - yes, but there are only two genders (good point) (I wonder where the brackets end?) (continued from "womankind"...cut down the rain forest (by the way, how many brackets can you have within other brackets?)))))))

After not figuring out the bracket issue, Doy and Bog decided to go to the park and walk each other. When they arrived, they began to throw a Frisbee back and forth. Just then a scientist walked up to the boys and said, "Did you know there is no greater force in the universe than the force that attracts a Frisbee to the exact center of the underneath a car?!!!" The scientist began to laugh hysterically.

"What a relief, I thought I was just imagining that," Doy said.

"It's a joke," said Bog.

CHAPTER FOR
Swimming with the Miami Dolphins

The next day Armageddon happened. After that Doy and Bog went swimming with the dolphins. This was not at some fancy resort in the Bahamas but at the city zoo. The dolphins were friendly and gave Doy and Bog some fish to eat.

"Boy, how do you guys eat fish all day?"

"Well it's filled with omega fatty acids which are really good for you." Dolphin 1 said.

"You guys are really good swimmers – it must be fun to jump out of the water like you do?"

"Is that a comment or a question?" Dolphin 2 asked.

"More of a comment."

"Oh…" Dolphin 2 replied.

"What I really liked is when you guys killed the Pittsburgh Steelers in the Super Bowl that one time."

"What the hell are you talking about?" Dolphin 1 queried.

"You know…oh wait, sorry, I meant that time you guys beat the Washington Redskins in the Super Bowl and you were undefeated."

"Oh, yeah, that was a great game." Dolphin 2 said.

"I mean that was incredible. How did you guys do it?"

"Well it wasn't easy but we really relied on the running game. In fact, if you like you can talk with Larry Csonka."

"Really, Larry Csonka is here?"

"Yes."

In the far side of the pool, what appears to be a large dolphin is swimming up to Doy and Bog. The dolphin stops and then takes its fake dolphin head off.

"Wow it's really Larry Csonka!!!" Bog yelled.

"You know…since this happened back in 1973 this skit is really outdated." Doy said sadly and then peed in the pool.

CHAPTER FIBE
The Call Center

The next year, Doy and Bog got jobs at a nearby call center. They were trained on selling farmasuticals.

"Good day, thank you for calling the call center. My name is Bog, how can I help you today?"

"Yes, I am interested in losing some weight."

"Have you thought about shooting off your head? Sorry, just a little levity."

There's silence on the other end of the phone.

"Anyway, yes, we do have a pill that will allow you to lose over one hundred pounds in less than three minutes."

"Wow, that sounds fantastic. I'm currently on welfare and only have five dollars."

"Really? How much do you weigh?"

"Well about five hundred and thirty-eight."

"So if you are on welfare how do you afford food?"

"Well with food stamps I can only afford a few things so I get cocoa-puffs, fried chicken, potatoes, sugar smacks and licorice. You know, the five food groups?"

"Hmmm, I see. I imagine you could also use some pills to prevent diabetes?"

"Yes. It's a sad commentary on contemporary life isn't?"

"Yeah, you might as well get a gun and kill yourself. Well anyway, have a great day and thank you for calling the call center."

Meanwhile, across the call center floor, Doy is about to take a call.

Ring, ring, ring, ring, ring, ring, ring.

"Thank you for calling the call center, this is Doy, how can I help you?"

"Yes, I just want to voice a complaint about the last call. I think it in poor taste that Bog should put down someone on welfare."

"Sorry, ma'am…"

"Sir!"

"Sorry sir but the last call was written to be a little dark."

"Well, I find it in poor taste!!!"

"Well thank you for telling me your comments"

"Oh, and by the way, I just got more with GEICO."

"Okay, get off the phone."

The call center that the boys were working in was the type that would take calls for many corporations. One of the company's they worked for was Fresh Air, an airline that flew within the United States.

Ring, ring, ring, ring, ring, ring, ring

"Good afternoon and thank you for calling Fresh Air, this is Bog, how can I help you?"

"Yes, I am interested in flying to Syracuse."

"Yes, sir and what day would you like to leave?"

"How about this Friday?"

"Certainly sir. And where will you be leaving from?"

"Memphis."

"Very good sir, we do have a flight leaving Memphis at 10 am and arriving into Syracuse at 12 noon."

"Wow, that's a short flight."

"Yes, well it's not that far between Tennessee and New York."

"Tennessee and New York?!!! I don't want to fly between Tennessee and New York! I want to fly between Egypt and Sicily!"

"Well, we do not fly to those destinations. Besides which, it does take about the same amount of time to fly between Tennessee and New York as it does to fly between Egypt and Sicily."

"Oh yea, I guess it does. So much for that joke. Anyway, I also need to make a trip next month."

"Yes sir, and where do you need to fly to and from?"

"I need to go from Toledo, Ohio to Toledo, Spain."

"That is also not very funny besides Toledo Spain is pronounced Toe–lay-do, not Toe-lee-do."

"Okay, how about this. Portland Oregon to Portland Maine?"

"No."

"How 'bout Minneapolis to Acropolis via Indianapolis?"

"No."

"How 'bout Pittsburgh to Vicksburg?"

"No."

"How 'bout Paris, California to Paris, France?"

"No."

"How 'bout Washington state to Washington D.C.?"

"No."

"How 'bout Green Bay, Wisconsin to Greenville, South Carolina?"

"Now that we do."

"Great, how much are the tickets?"

"1200 dollars."

"Wow, I just want a seat not the whole plane!"

"If you wanted to buy the whole plane it would be $22 million dollars."

"Isn't there anything cheaper than $1200?"

"Well, we do have a fare for $500."

"Well, that's a bit better. What do I have to do to get that deal?"

"Well, you can only fly on Tuesday. You have to wear a purple shirt and sit on your head the entire flight. Oh, and one last thing – you have to memorize the entire story of "A Tale of Two Cities," by Charles Dickens and then recite it to one of the flight attendants."

"What if I memorized "A City of Two Tales," by Darl Chickens instead?"

"Well, that book doesn't exist."

"No, you don't exist!"

And with that the conversation went into non-existence.

CHAPTER STIX
Poetry

Doy and Bog were looking through some books discussing poetry and how they felt about it. They typically felt with their hands but today they were going to feel with their feelings – they wanted to get emotional.

"Okay Bog, there's a poem I remember from my childhoop that I think will inspire you. It goes like this…

How do I love thee? Let me count the waves.
I love thee to the depth and breadth and height and width and length my tape measure can reach,
when feeling out of sight baby
For the maps of Bing and ideal face.
I love thee to the level of every day's
Most quiet sneeze, by sun and candle-light.
I pee freely, as men strive for right.
I love thee pureed, and placed you in a stew.
I love thee with a passionfruit
In my old briefs that I need to change.
I love thee with a love I seemed to snooze
With my lost saints. I love thee with halotosis,

Smiles, beers, of all my life; and, if God choose,
I shall but love thee to death (I'm a big nag).

"Wow Doy, that was magic."

"Thanks Bog. How 'bout you read me something from that poetry book?"

"Sounds good Doy. Oh here's one. Are you ready?"

"Yes."

"You sure?"

"Yes, I'm quite sure."

"I just want to make sure you are absolutely ready?"

"Yes, I am absolutely ready."

"Good, because I am about to begin."

"Great."

"Here we go."

"Terrific."

Several hours later…

"This a poem by Steven Robert Louison. And here it goes…

How do I count thee? Let me love the ways.
I count thee to infinity plus one.
I count thee like a bag of chips and all that.
If you were a cow I would slaughter thee with my counting ability.

If you were a piece of cake I would eat you
until every last morsel was counted…and
then I would vomit.
If you were a pile of rocks, I would count you
over and over until I threw you into the sea.
If you were a bunch of kindling wood, I would
count you until you were burnt up in the fire.
If you were a Flock of Seagulls I would listen
to your CD.
If you were a pod of whales, I would buy you
an iPod.
If you were 12-inch ruler, I would count every
sixteenth of you.
You have been officially counted!!!

CHAPTER SEBEN
The Election

Doy and Bog found work at the campaign headquarters of Jimothy Swift. Jimothy was running for his life. He was also running for dictator for the city of Rutherford.

The boys threw themselves into their work and then once they had been thrown, got up and dusted themselves off. They really enjoyed the work. They did stick drawings of Swift for posters and hung them around town. They put together an interesting puppet show that showed the citizens of Rutherford what a truly despotic person Swift really was. But best of all they got to write his speeches. And so, at the next campaign rally, Jimothy Swift gave his last speech.

"Good evening ladies and germs. I say germs because there are a lot of germs in this building, not because it is an old vaudeville joke. I'm basically a germaphobe. And what better way to make sure your city is clean by hiring a homophobe…excuse me, I mean germaphobe. I hobe that we can all get over our hobes and really become great ben and vimin we can be probed of.

About three thousand years ago, Hammering Hank Aaron hit his record-breaking home run defeating Babe Ruth in the bottom of the 9th. He then ate Babe Ruth…I mean the candy bar not the guy with the weird name. Anyway, it was a great story about overcoming the odds, overcoming hatred and bigotry. And I want to do that today…overcoming odds I mean not eating candy. And so, I ask that you consider me for your city dictator. I will rule with an iron fist. Here is my agenda as city dictator…

First, I will invade our neighbor Poland Estates. Then I will flatten French Gardens and then destroy England and Sons Law Firm. Next I will conquer Russian River Canoe and Boating Supply. From there I will rule over the entire state of New Jersey which includes all the Starbucks…I do enjoy a delicious expresso.

And so in conclusion, why have a dictator if he won't take decisive action and destroy his enemies!"

And so, the next day Jimothy lost the election. It turns out he was running for city council and not city dictator.

CHAPTER ATE
Outer Space

On the 32nd of October, something something, Doy and Bog passed their astronaut exams. They thought they were taking an exam to become bank tellers but the testing lady got the tests mixed-up. Later that day she fell into a hole and was never heard from again. Her husband took a search party with him to try and find her but they all fell into the same hole and were never heard from again. After hearing this news, the local police department was notified of the incident and they began to investigate. They too fell into the hole and were never heard from again…and so on and so on.

On March the 2nd, five hundred years later, Doy and Bog marched into the NASA headquarters. They wore their best suit which was a shame because only one person could fit into it and it was now really wrinkled. They met with the Star Fleet Commander of NASA named Mr. Spork. Mr. Spork ordered Doy and Bog do a series of mental and physical tests before they could "fly the rocket". Doy and Bog refused to take the tests on the grounds that they might incriminate them and so Mr. Spork gave them their wings.

“Now, before ‘you fly the rocket’…” Mr. Spork said, using his fingers to make air quotes, “I want you to look at this poster.”

Doy and Bog complied and looked at the poster. The poster was black with some small white spots on it.

“This boys…this is space.” Mr. Spork then began to cry. He was soon on his knees weeping. He finally pulled himself together because he had broken in to smaller pieces.

“Now, I want you to get out there and ‘fly the rocket’!” he again said with air quotes.

Just then a sliding door opened and two men in white lab coats ushered Doy and Bog into a room that looked like a laboratory.

“Boys, my name is ring leader 52 and I want to wish you all the best on your journey. I look forward to you both ‘flying the rocket.’” He said with a smile to his colleague. A look that both Doy and Bog could not ignore.

“Why does everyone keep referring to “flying the rocket’ with air quotes?” Bog asked.

The two men shook their heads in confusion.

“Anyway, I know this is ‘your big day’…” this time ring leader 53 used air quotes.

“…but we are all ‘rooting for you’.”

Doy and Bog ignored the constant air quotes and began to suit up in their astronaut get-ups.

"Okay, now through 'that door', you will find the 'rocket ship'." Ring leader 52 said as he patted the two on their backs.

Just as the ring leader said, there in front of the boys as they walked out of the NASA headquarters was a Saturn VI rocket. It looked glorious in the morning sun. The herons were chirping; the gators were burping and the flamingos were going. The two stood awestruck at what they were seeing. From the doorway to the headquarters stood the two lab assistants.

"When you get to the capsule, just hit the red button and you will be on 'your way'." Both said in unison and with air quotes.

Doy and Bog shook their heads and then took the elevator to the top of the rocket. They opened the hatch and strapped themselves into their seats. Another man in a lab coat gave them the thumbs up and closed the hatch behind him.

In the tower next to the launch pad, a rather obese man in glasses began the countdown.

"One million."

"Nine hundred and ninety nine thousand, nine hundred and ninety nine…"

"I think you can start from ten Bill." A rather perturbed janitor sweeping the floor said to the NASA technician.

"Oh okay, Louie. I mean it's not like I went to engineering school for four years and grad school and got my Phd, and worked endless hours of overtime, went through a divorce to get to this position…"

"Oh good, because I would have hated to know that you just wasted your life." Louie left with a smile and a skip in his step. Bill shook his head and started the countdown again.

"Ten, nine, eight, seven, six, five, four, three, two one, ignition, lift-off!"

Unable to hear Bill, Doy and Bog just sat in the space capsule. About five minutes later they just hit the red button and the spacecraft was soon lifting off the Launchpad at the John's Bones Space Center in Hewton, Texas.

The space flight was incredible for the boys. They could see the moon fly by and then they hurtled past Mars. After lunch they could see Jupiter outside of their window. Before they knew it, Saturn whizzed by. They made fun of Your anus and were soon skimming the atmosphere of Neptune. They were amazed to see Pluto white and cold and offered to send it a blanket. When they reached the Kuiper Belt they decided to have dinner. As they passed by Alpha Centuri they knew they had flown over 7,000,000,000,000,000,000,000,000,000,000,000,000,000,000,000,000,000,000,000,000,000,000,000,000,000,000,000,000,000,000,000,000,000,000,000,000,000,000,000,000,000,000,000,000,000,000,000,000,000,000,000,000,000,000,000,000,000,000,

000,000,000,000,000,000,000,000,000,000,000,0
00,000,000,000,000,000,000,000,000,000,000,00
0,000,000,000,000,000,000,000,000,000,000,000,
000,000,000,000,000,000,000,000,000,000,000,0
00,000,000,000,000,000,000,000,000,000,000,00
0,000,000,000,000,000,000,000,000,000,000,000,
000,000,000,000,000,000,000,000,000 'miles', at least according to the odometer. They had even passed Voyager 1 and Voyager 2, New Horizons and Apollo 5.

Doy's and Bog's spaceflight was incredible, but they finally ran out of space and crashed into a big wall.

"Hewton, we have a problem."

"My name is Bill. What do you need?"

"Well, we've run out of space."

"Really, I thought that was impossible?"

"Well, we are staring at it. It's a big #4@#%!&#! Wall!"

"Hmmmm."

"Any ideas Bill?"

"Hmmmm. No, not a one."

The boys examined the space ship further and could see that the communications antenna at the top of the space capsule was stuck in the wall and it would be impossible to pull it out. They instead hailed a cab and headed home.

CHAPTER NIFE
The Washdisher

Doy was starting to get upset with Bog as he felt he was the one that always had to do the dishes.

"Hey Bog, you left your dirty plates in the sink again. Why can you clean them up?"

"C'mon Doy, it's too much work. Let's just do it at the end of the week."

"End of the week. This sink will be overflowing!"

"No it won't, we don't do that much eating."

"Well, if we don't do that much eating then it shouldn't take long to rinse off your dishes and place them in the washdisher."

"Frankly it does take too much time. You forget that I'm quite busy."

"Really?"

"Yes really."

"Really?'

"Yes really."

"Really?" (Said it a very sarcastic voice)

"Yes really."

"Really? (Said in an even more sarcastic voice)

"Yes really."

"Really?" (Said in an even more sarcastic voice than the time just before)

"Yes really."

"Really?" (Said in an extremely sarcastic voice that was so high-pitched only certain bogs could hear it)

"Yes. Today I am going parasailing, then I am going to deliver a speech to congress regarding the recent epidemic in overuse of emojis for texting, then I am playing Hai lai, then I am going to my Kazakstan language lesson, then I am going skiing, then I am going hox funting…"

"Wait, don't you men fox hunting?"

"Yeah right. Anyway, the I am going to do some refrigeration repair over at my grandmother's house, then I will do some boating, then an hour of gee jit su, then fifteen minutes of exercise over at the infirmary, then five hours of megatation, then ten hours of grocery shopping, then ninety hours of deep reflection…"

"You know there are only twenty-four hours in a day?"

"Yeah, right, then I am going swimming, then I am going to do some pay cligeon shooting, then I am going to study the Russian Revolution…"

"Okay, I get it. You're busy. Anyway, at the very most it only takes five minutes to clean-up what is typically in the sink."

"Yeah right."

"Don't believe me? Why don't we do a time study?"

"A time study?"

"Yes, a time study."

"A time study?"

"Why do I get the feeling you're stalling."

"Why do you get the feeling…"

"SHUT UP!!!! Now go upstairs and get the watchstop."

"What's a watchstop?"

"It's a watch that stops time. When you stop time it tells you how long something has taken."

"Ok, sounds good. I'll take the escalator."

Since there wasn't really an escalator, bog went behind the couch and then slowly raised himself from a crouching position, giving the appearance that he was rising up an escalator.

"Are you done?"

"Yes."

Bog proceeded to go upstairs and seven years later reappeared with the watchstop. In the time it took him to retrieve the watch, several administrations and empires had risen and fallen. Ruth Babe finally broke the record for most Runshome. She was a fine woman.

"Boy, time really stands still when you try to accomplish something bog."

"Why thank you doy."

"Okay, now, you take everything that is in the sink and place it into the washdisher, and then I will time you."

"Why me? Why don't you do it?"

"Fine, I will put the dishes into the washdisher and you use the watchstop to time me."

"Great."

"Okay, ready?"

"Ready."

"Go!"

Doy proceeded to put all the plates and dishes and silverware into the washdisher. He did so in a very efficient and methodical manner.

"Done! What was my time?"

"I don't know. I don't know how to read this thing."

"Look, your supposed to hold the watchstop on the tip of your finger. You then move in a circle around the watchstop. Each revolution is about a second and then you count each revolution."

"Wouldn't it be easier just to count?"

"Yes, I suppose it would."

Doy then threw the watchstop into the wall where it exploded into a million pieces. Doy then took all of the plates and silverware out of the washdisher and assembled them in a pile in the sink.

"Ok, so are you ready Bog?"

"Yes Doy."

"Begin."

"1, 2, 3, 4ourp…"

"What is 4ourp?"

"Sorry, I meant to say 4."

"Did you mean to say 4 or four?"

"Does it make a difference? Don't they sound the same?"

"Yes, but it looks different when it's written down."

"Is all of this going to be written down?"

"Perhaps."

"Is someone writing this down now?"

"I don't know. Maybe there's someone right now writing it down."

"Who? Where?"

"Maybe it's a Russian spy. Maybe they're hiding behind that wall over there and they are listening to our conversation."

"Really?"

"Yes really."

"So you are saying that someone from Russia has come and planted themselves secretively behind one of our walls and is listening to our conversation on how to create a time-study on how quickly it takes to put away the dishes?"

"Perhaps. Maybe they want to know how people from our country wash dishes and the methods we employ."

At that point Doy and Bog began to look around the house to see if there was a Russian spy. Several days later they determined that there were no spies. They then returned to their time study.

"Ok ready?"

"Ready."

"Go."

Doy proceeded to put the dishes away while Bog counted.

"237…"

"And done. So, it took 237 seconds or 3 minutes and 57 seconds."

"That's not correct. It took 3 days, five hours and 38 seconds."

"How do you mean?"

"Well, when you told me to start counting we were in the middle of a discussion on whether or not there was a Russian spy in the house."

"So?"

"So, I was counting the whole time like you told me."

"You were?"

"Yes. Silently to myself."

"Well, that is something. Anyway, just subtract all of that Russian spy time stuff and you arrive at 3 minutes and 57 seconds to put away the dishes. So why can't you put away the dishes?"

"Because like always there some espinoge or something going on that makes washing the dishes take a long time and just don't have time for it."

"Look, you just need to isolate the activity of washdishing to the time that you actually take the dishes out of the sink and place them in the washdisher. It's that simple."

"Oh, that I wish it were Doy, or how I wish it were."

At that point Doy began to look off into the distance and Bog jumped out of the kitchen window.

CHAPTER TENT
Loots and Shatters

Doy and Bog began a play-rolling club in Central Park with their friends. They used to play Bludgeon and Bagels but they got tired of that and started a new game they called Loots and Shatters.

Doy and Bog and their five million and two friends, would gather in Central Park. Luckily, Central Park had a capacity of five million and three, but they couldn't find the additional friend. It was probably because he was hiding. Anyway, they would gather every third Saturday to engage in this trilling but dull battle of wits and senses.

The object of the game was to break into someone's imaginary house and loot their valuables. Since technically you needed to shatter a window of someone's house before looting them, the name should really be Shatters and Loots, but it is not as funny based on the whole concept of this book being about re-arranging words differently.

Doy loved playing Candyland and Shoots and Ladders as young commodore and later he really enjoyed Bunjuns and Banjos and so he decided to create a special play-rolling game as previously mentioned above.

"Okay everyone, do you have your windows ready?"

"No, I couldn't find one!" yelled Paul at the top of his lungs. He later tried yelling at the bottom of his lungs but that didn't help.

"Can someone lend this poor sod a window?"

"I can!" yelled Peter.

"So this is robbing Peter to pay Paul," Bog began to laugh.

"Just shut-up Bog!!! Okay everyone begin!"

As they began to play or roll, as the case maybe, Doy noticed a young lady sitting on a rock. She seemed sad and wasn't participating in the game.

"Hi, don't you want to play in the game?"

"I would but I don't have a partner. It's a very sad story."

"Why don't you tell me about it?"

And so the young lady named Bongolyn relayed the entire story of her life in matter of 13 minutes. She came from a long line of large cement commercial warehouse prefabricators. When she was 8 years old she was forced to work long hours at a health spa where she was given delicious food and made to splash around in a lagoon-shaped pool. When she grew tired of that she was then forced to listen to her favorite music for the rest of the day. She absolutely hated it.

The real sad part of her life came later when she met her boyfriend Tombon. Tombon was the most handsome boy in the entire northeast corner of the health spa. He had blue-green eyes, golden hair, big muscles and the ability to pack unusually large items inside of smaller suitcases. After a short courtship, they were engaged to be married, but the following month Tombon was killed in a tragic water-balloon accident.

"I'm so sorry to hear that Bongolyn. That must have been difficult."

"Yes it was a freak accident. Not many people drown during a water-balloon fight."

It was at this point that Doy began to study the sky and hum.

"I think the best thing for you is to join in the fun. You will get lost in the world of Loots and Shatters."

Bongolyn began to move the dirt at her feet around, trying to decide if she wanted to play or to continue moving the dirt around. She enjoyed moving the dirt around.

"C'mon, let's play!"

Bongolyn relented and joined in the fun. Doy gave her a window with which she took a large sledgehammer and smashed it to pieces. She then stepped through the window and found a young man on a make believe bed (really lying on the grass).

"Hey what are you doing here?"

"Quiet!"

Bongolyn then proceeded to gag and bag the young man. Before bagging him, she pulled out his wallet and began to count the loot.

"Well done Bongolyn! How much did you loot?"

"I have twenty dollars and ten cents!"

"Great, now you can buy yourself a Barstucks coffee."

The games continued for another 12 hours and a total of three trillion dollars and ten cents was looted. It had been a productive day.

CHAPTER LEBEN
Carpool Tunnel Vision

Doy and Boy received employment at a local computer store. They would be there to set-up computers and confront the Internet. Their boss was Casbah the Friendly Web Host. Since the three of them lived in the same fort together, they decided they would commute to work in their carbuncle.

One day the main road to work was out and they had to take a country road. The road was pretty…well the road wasn't pretty but the scenery around the road was pretty…well it was average. Anyway, they took the windy road that made its ways through the mountains and Starbucks. At one point the mountains were so high that they had to go through a long tunnel. It was dark in the tunnel and the boys were starting to get a little sick as the car weaved in and out of traffic. Casbah was at the wheel and since he didn't know how to drive, it made their commute very hair-raising.

At one point the boys got so sick they had to vomit out the window. This was unfortunate because there was a howling wind driving down the tunnel and when they threw-up the vomit splattered all over them. Doy suggested that he take over the driving duties and Casbah yielded to his request. After switching pilots, Doy drew a long breath and accelerated down the road.

As they made their way down the tunnel they realized that what they were driving through was not so much a tunnel as it was a portal into time. With each mile, they would enter a new epoch. First it was oughts, then the nineties, then the eighties, the cool seventies, the swinging sixties, the fifties, and so on. As they entered the roaring twenties they could also see that their car changed into a Model-T, then they were on a locomotive, and then horseback. They finally arrived in what appeared to be Paris in 1799 during the French Revolution.

"Hey, is that Marie Antoinette?" Bog asked.

"I think it is," said Doy.

"Hey, look, she's eating cake," Casbah retorted.

They pulled their horses over and began to engage the French monarch.

"Hello, your heinous…"

"That's your highness, ding-dong!"

Marie Antoinette began to laugh. "Ilsont de bon bon?" She asked.

"What?"

"Ilsont de bon bon?"

"You moron, she only speaks French."

"Oh. Well, how do we learn French so we can speak with her?"

"I've got my cell-phone, maybe I can use Google Translate?" Bog suggested.

"Great idea!"

"Oh, I don't seem to have any service."

The trio began to survey the scene and started to look for a school where they could learn French. They went into a café and asked the waitress.

"Madame, do you know of a school where we can learn French?"

"Poulve francaise, mounsuer?" She asked.

"Hmmm, this is going to be difficult. How can we learn French if we can't get anyone to understand us?"

"You know, the English Channel is close by. Maybe we can take a boat over to England, get someone there who understands French and come back and find us a school that teaches French?"

"Well, if they speak French, why would we need to go to a school to learn French? They could translate for us. But I like your plan of going over to England."

The trio took a flying saucer to the Dunkirk. From there they took a sailing saucer and landed on Plymouth Rock several days later.

"Wow, that was quite the trip."

"Agreed, now let's see if we can find someone who can speak French."

"Excuse me sir, but do you know anyone who speaks French?"

"We we."

"The bathroom is over there," Bog pointed to a sandcastle near the beach.

"No, I mean I speak ze French."

"Really. I detect more of a Bulgarian accent. Can you prove it?'

"Yes, here are all my documents proving that I can speak ze French."

The man produced a large box of documents that if you lined them one on top of the other they would stretch to Mars.

"I noticed that each document has the words 'he speaks ze French' and what appears to be melted crayon used as a type of stamp?"

"We, each one of these 87 million documents are proof that I can speak ze the French."

At that point Doy and Bog took the man across the channel and began to scour the entire city of Paris for a school that taught people to how to speak French. They visited every nook and cranny. They visited every atom and molecule. They left no stone unturned which really made the Parisians angry as they didn't like their stones turned. Eventually they finally found one. It was called the "How to Learn French in Five Easy Lessons," store.

CHAPTER TWELFTH

House Roughing

Boy and Dog recently became realtors. Of course the National Realty Association didn't know so no harm, no foul. The boys put on their gold, pink and gray cardigans and began to walk the streets looking for potential buyers of homes.

"Say Mr. and Mrs........"

"Smith," A large man in a green cardigan said.

"Say Mr. and Mrs. Smith, we'd like to sell you that house over there. Would you like to buy it?"

"Why yes we would. How much?"

"We can let you have that baby for just one thousand bucks!"

"What that is quite a deal, don't you think so honey?"

The beautiful brunette woman in a pink cardigan began to nod her head incessantly.

"Well here's a contract and a pen to sign it."

The man signed the contract and handed the boys $1,000 in new one dollar bills.

"Congratulations on becoming new homeowners. We'll see yah later."

"Wait. Don't we need the keys?"

"Actually, just go inside and the people who are showing the house will give you the keys."

"Excellent. Thanks boys!"

Running hand in hand, the man with the green cardigan and the beautiful brunette woman in a pink cardigan ran into their new house which really hurt since the front door wasn't open. When they did open the front door they were greeted by an elderly couple.

"Who are you?" As the new homeowner man in a green cardigan.

"Why we are the Greens," said the elderly woman who was wearing a yellow cardigan.

"Well, we just bought this house," said the beautiful brunette woman in the pink cardigan.

"Oh no, I think you have been fooled by Doy and Bog. They're a couple of crazy kids who dress up like realtors and keep selling our house to strangers."

At that point everyone had a good laugh until they didn't.

The pair of couples then picked up the house and threw it at Doy and Bog striking them square in the head. Doy and Bog took the house and then sold it to another couple who were shopping for houses until the whole cycle of selling the house, being duped and then throwing the house at the boys happened over and over again until the story finally finished.

CHAPTER UNLUCKY NUMBER THIRPTEEN

Words

Once Ponce DeLeon Tyme, there were two boys named Doy and Bog. They liked to use their words…

"Bog, I think it's time that we cut to the chase until the cows come home. What say you man?"

"Well, I simply succinctly seriously say that without a dubious doubt about it that without a hair of concern or a feeling of regret that without remorse or remodeling glue, that in fact without a morsel of concealment and I am completely prepared to say that I am inside of my brain right now examining each neuron and molecule and atom that is going back and forth and creating an electrical impulse that is telling my tongue to move in an up and down motion that causes a vibration that causes a sound to emanated from my mouth and travel to your ear and which makes me wonder that if a tree were to fall in a forest and no one was there would anyone really care?"

"Well, said my friend. I think we are ready for our interview with the wordsmith."

"Me three!"

Jonathan Wordsmith was looking for two people to help him in his quest to create words. The boys saw this online advertisement for a word creator and immediately high-tailed it over to Wordsmith's office. The office was closed however and so they had to come back the following Tuesday. Before they met with Wordsmith they decided to practice their "wording." Having tested each other for days they met with Wordsmith at his high-rise office near the basement.

"Hello, my name is Doy and this is my associate Bog."

"Hello and nice to meet you. My name is Katrina Rezvlvlylvzlyvzlvyllszzlllyvk."

"Nice to meet you Katrina ah…ah, Katrina R. We have an appointment with Messrs Wordsmith."

"Excellent gentlemen. Please go to conference room 47 and he will meet you there shortly."

"As long as it isn't longly," Bog said with a bright smile.

"Oh, I see what you mean. Ha ha ha ha ha ha ha ha ha ha ha ha ha ha ha ha ha ha ha ha ha ha ha ha ha ha ha ha ha ha ha (The woman continues to ha-ha incessantly for several hours.)

The boys quickly found room 47 after they had explored rooms 1, 2, 3, 4, 5, Seis, 7, 200, 8,

72, 9, 19, 21, 52, Valentino, 31, Bath, 15, 16, Living, 22, 23, Bed, 41, 42, 39, Piper, 17, 18, 24, 25, Stock, 26, 28, 14, 13, 11, Dining, 20, 30, 717, 44, 33, 35, 34, 45, Rumpus, 10, 46, 40, Tasting, 31, 32, 12, 27, 29, 39, 37, 38 and 43, but not necessarily in that order. (For those of you playing at home, we have thrown in the words "Valentino" and "Piper" to throw you off the scent. ☺)

"Good afternoon gentlemen, allow me to introduce myself. I am Harold A. Wordsmith. Welcome to my fine establishment."

"This is very factorory Mr. Wordsmith." Bog said shaking his hand and wearing a maniacal look on his face.

"Ah very good Mr. Bog, I see you have been inventing words."

"Oh yes very so much." Bog's brain began melting inside of its cranium.

"Well, please don't hurt yourself on my account. I know inventing words can sometimes cause your brain to spring a leak but you don't have to break it on my account. And you must be Mr. Doy?"

"Yes I am. And may I say that I feel very fluvescent today."

"Excellent. I like where you two are going with this. Now, I would like to get down to business and do some smithwording."

"Don't you mean wordsmithing?"

"No, I just got the rightcopy for smithwording."

"Oh, I see," said Bog.

"What is rightcopy?' asked Doy.

"Rightcopy is my copyright for someone who possesses the right copy of the work."

"Ah, I get it!" said Bog shaking his head.

"So, do you own the copyright for rightcopy as well?" Doy asked.

"Funny you should ask that but sadly no. You see I went to the copyright office and said I'd like to fill out an application to copyright rightcopy. The man behind the desk was feeling ill and was not comprehending my meaning."

"When I meet people like that I immediately ask for their Super vizor."

"Super vizor?"

"Yes, that's one of my other made up words. I like to uze the letter Z as often az I can you zee?"

"Yes, I get your driftz."

"So then what happened?"

"Well I talked with a Ms. Chumley who told me that it was impossible to get a copyright on rightcopy because they do not copyright words. They only copyright various works like novels and plays, etc."

"What is e-t-c?" (Bog is employing this question as if he can read what the author is currently writing. I wonder if he can see what I am writing right now? Ohhh that would be vexing."

"Etc., stands for et cetera, or meaning that there is something similar that would further follow."

"Oh, yes of course, how silly of me, et cetera."

"I don't think you are using that correctly?"

"Oh I think I am et cetera."

"So you mean that you are saying something similar is to follow when you say 'how silly of me'?"

"Yes of course, you know like 'how silly of me,' and then I would say 'what an idiot I am being,' or 'how on earth can anyone be more of a moron than me," et cetera."

At that point Wordsmith began to look around the room for anything he could hang himself with.

"Bog, please, can't you see you are annoying Mr. Wordsmith?"

Bog agreed and began to look around the room for anything he could hang himself with.

"So continue Mr. Wordsmith."

"Yes, so Ms. Chumley told me that words are a part of language and you cannot copyright them."

"But what about Kleenex?"

"Well that's a brand name. You can copyright brand names."

"No I mean do you have any Kleenex. I have a runny nose."

"Oh I say, so it is."

Both Doy and Mr. Wordsmith begin to look at Bog with an expression of horror as his nose was becoming unusually watery. Mr. Wordsmith grabbed a box of ~~Kleenex~~ nose papers and handed them to Bog. Bog immediately took out the pieces of paper and wiped his nose with them.

"Say, that gives me an idea of a word. How about 'noseyrun,'?"

"That is a good one Doy."

"Yes, it does imply that you have a runny nose. Good one! I'll write it down."

"Now getting back to Ms. Chumley. Was she married?"

Doy elbowed Bog in his arm signaling that the question was inappropriate.

"Actually, I meant to say, if she says that words cannot be copyrighted, then all the words we come up with today could be plagiarized?"

"Yes that's true."

"So what's the point?"

"I guess there really isn't one."

"Okay, I guess we'll be seeing you Mr. Wordsmith."

"Bye boys."

Doy and Bog begin to walk out of the room. Bog begins to think. He looks up and then stares out of a nearby window. He then walks back into Mr. Wordsmith's office.

"Mr. Wordsmith?"

"Yes, my dear chap?"

"Do you happen to have Ms. Chumley's number?"

CHAPTER FORETEEN

Doy and Bog's Top Ten Things to Watch out for or to Avoid.

10: Great White Sharks in your Coffee!!!

9: Baseball Bats!!!

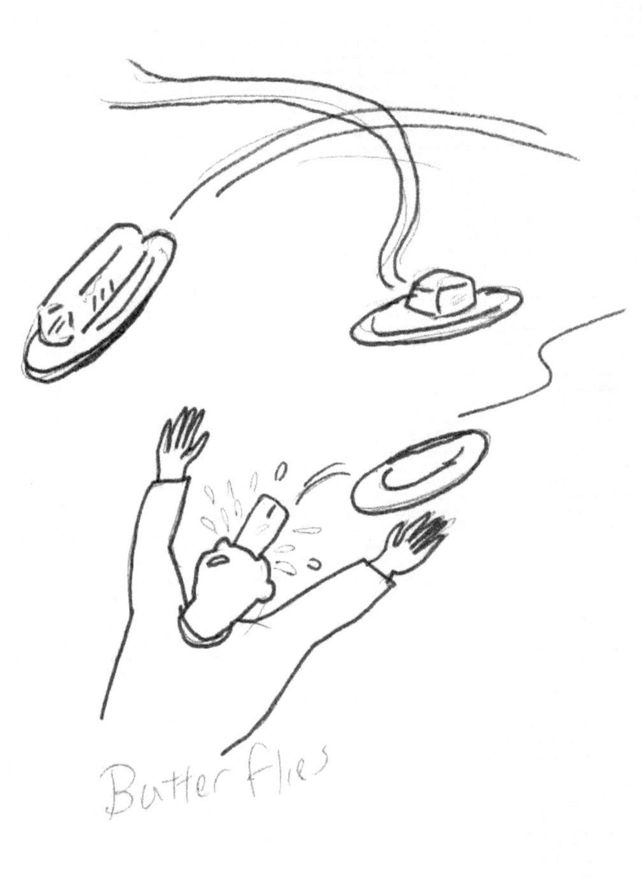

8: Butterflies

7: Computer Viruses

6: Long Walks on Short Piers

5: Indoor Trampolines

4: Peanut Butter and Jelly Fish

3: Gas Leaks at the Plant

2: Losing Your Train of Thought

And the Number 1 thing that Doy and Bog recommend that you watch out for or to avoid…

Whale Wells!!!

CHAPTER FLIPTEEN
Standdown Comedy

Doy and Bog challenged each other as to whom had the best sense of humor. They decided to go to the amateur hour at the local comedy super store. It was a dark and seedy place where a lot of plants grew…because it was moist and it was dark and seedy. You know like plant seeds…duh!!! Anyway, there was smoke in the air and the sound of cocktail glasses clinking. Waiters and waitresses were moving around aimlessly and molecules were trapped in their aura. Many of them were struggling actors and came to work on Bill's Comedy Super Store because, well, they were struggling actors and weren't very good, except when they had to the utility companies and pretend they were unable to pay their bills. Which they were really not able to pay their bills so they were not really acting anyway. Anywho, it was a wonderful night. The sky was clear and there were no clouds in the ceiling.

Bog went first, after the stage manager threw him out there.

"Good evening ladies and germs. I would address the gentlemen but I can tell by the hygiene of this place there are a lot of germs." (Off stage the sound of a drumstick hitting a snare drum and then a cymbal is heard. Then there is the sound of crickets chirping).

"Anyway. How about socks? What's up with those? Can you ever get a pair to come out of the dryer? Am I right, am I right?" (Off stage the sound of a drumstick hitting a snare drum and then a cymbal is heard. Then there is the sound of crickets whispering to each other.)

"And how about you ladies? Am I right? What's up with that? Am I right?" (Off stage the sound of a drumstick hitting a snare drum and then a cymbal is heard. Then there is the sound of crickets constructing a small replica city of Troy. They are using very small bulldozers, cranes and dump trucks which creates significate noise.

"Anyway, you all have been great! Drive safe and make sure to tip your waiters and waitresses!!!"

Bog dropped his mic in triumph and then ran off the stage and into a vat of boiling cement. Doy was then called up on stage.

"Good evening ladles and germs. Yes, I'm speaking to you germs!!! he, he, he. (Off stage the sound of a drumstick hitting a snare drum and then a cymbal is heard. The replica city of Troy built by the crickets has caught on fire. Someone who is smoking in the audience has flicked some of their ash on to the replica. The crickets have called the local cricket fire department and a very small fire truck has been called to the scene.)

"You know, I was expecting a letter from my granny as it was the anniversary of the excavation of the lost City of Troy. She usually sends me some money on such momentous occasions. Anyway, she called me and said that she had mailed it the week previous as she wanted to arrive on the anniversary. Anyway, I decided to go to the post office and she what the issue was. When I got there I noticed that all of the staff was women! Can you believe it! Everyone knows that women can't do a mail (male) job!!!"

At that point, all the women in the audience stormed the stage. The drummer tried to hit the snare drum and then cymbal but he was bowled over by the large crowd of irate women. The crickets were smashed to bits as well. Doy and Bog began to run as fast as they could but the women easily caught them. They threw them into a large envelope, addressed it to the Taj Mahal, put the required postage on and then stuffed it into a nearby femail box. The boys arrived in India 23 years later. The local post office at the Taj Mahal noticed that there was insufficient postage and sent it back to the United States of Amiracle. The boys arrived somewhere near Antartica 10 years later. When they finally made it back to their house the boys were relieved.

"You know Bog, I really learned a lot about myself during that journey."

"Really, what's that Doy?"

"That women cannot do a mail (male) job!!!" The boys laughed incessantly as the closing credits started moving down the large TV screen.

CHAPTER SIXTYTEEN

Dogs – the musical

Doy and Bog decided to use their talents for musical theatre and put on production of *Dogs – the Musical* at their local department store. In this case, substitute spaghetti center for department store. Sorry scratch that, substitute theatre for spaghetti center. Sorry, substitute theater for theatre. What are we in bloody England!!!

Anyway, the boys looked forward to putting on their production. They hired people to build props and make costumes and draw baths, etc. After drawing baths they then drew backdrops for the stage. While all that was happening the boys wrote the script and created all the music for the production as there really wasn't a show called *Dogs -the Musical*. There was a show called *Cats* but Bog objected to that for obvious reasons, wink, wink, wink (imagine someone winking their right eye at that point. You can also imagine someone winking their right eye and then chewing gum as a substitute to the first imagining).

After a lot of hard work the boys were ready to open their show. During the first performance, a few things went wrong but overall it was a good performance. By a "few" things I mean everything; the costume designer showed up with wolverine costumes instead of dog costumes. The curtain would not go up, the members of the orchestra had a group migraine, most of the audience was made up of cats and the caterer for the after-show party heard the word "Styrofoam" instead of "spumoni." So what was originally conceived turned-out to be a loose collection of chaotic songs sung over a group of badgers running in and out of the main curtain with cats peeing all over the theatre. One critic said they couldn't even comment on the show because they were throwing up the whole time. One critic wrote…

In all my years in theatre (yes, that's spelled theatre), I have never heard such a psychotic noise emanating from the orchestra pit with what appeared to be an acid induced hallucination going on the stage behind them.

On the second night things went a little better as the theatre caught fire and burned down to the ground. *Dogs – the Musical* had come to an abrupt end.

CHAPTER SEVEN HEAVEN
You Can't Teach an Old Bog New Tricks

Doy and Bog decided that they needed to learn some sayings so they could become more socially acceptable at parties, sporting events and *Downtown Abby Character Dress-up Nights*.

"Say Bog, what sayings do you know?" Asked Doy.

"Well there's the one about the sows."

"Oh yeah, how's it go?"

"You can stay out all night until the sows come home."

"I think you mean cows."

"Why would cows come home?"

"Why would sows come home?"

"I don't know. Either way you are going to have a messy living room." Both of the boys began to laugh and laugh and then eventually they stopped.

"Here, let's go on the internet and see what we can find." The boys proceeded to go onto the internet. It was rough at first but as the internet began to slow down they were eventually able to hop on.

"Oh, how about this one... 'kill them with kindness.'"

"Hmmm, why would someone be killed by someone else being kind to them?"

"I don't know. Maybe someone was kind enough to dig a pool for someone, but the other someone accidently fell in it."

"Oh I see. Or maybe someone bought the other someone a new car but accidently drove over them?"

"Could be, could be."

"How about this one… 'I've got bigger fish to fry.'"

"Hmmm, sounds like someone bragging. I see your little fish frying but I've got bigger fish than yours that I can fry."

"Yes, I think you've got it Bog."

"Excellent. Let's learn a few more and I think we will be ready for tomorrow night's Edgar Allan Poe Dress-up Extravaganza and Ms. Lucy's house."

The boys spent the rest of the night learning more sayings and hopping around the internet wherever they could.

The following evening the boys arrived at precisely 9:13pm which was a shame since the event ended at 9:13pm. The boys wouldn't have to wait very long though as the following evening there was a Titanic Dress Up Evening at Ms.

Betsy's house. Doy came as Jack Dawson and Bog was Cyranno De Bergerec.

"Why you guys look great!" Ms. Betsy said to the boys.

"I'd like to introduce you to Mr. Phillip Barnweavil who is the head of Sanderson Soups. And he is dressed as Captain Smith."

"Abandon Ship!" Mr. Barnweavil yelled. Doy looked around in confusion while Bog hit the floor.

"Just kidding boys. Glad to meet you."

"The pleasure is all mine Mr. Barnweavil. That is a great costume."

"Why thank you. I had my auntie knit it all night."

"Until the cows came home?" Bog said winking and elbowing Mr. Barnweavil." Mr. Barnweavil smiled and then walked away.

"Oh and this is Dan Gladwell. He's dressed up as piece of wet furniture that has been thrown overboard."

"Good to meet you." Dan said as he they shook hands with his wet glove.

"One man's trash is another man's treasure." Doy said while nodding his head like a possessed jack-in-the-box.

"Oh ah, well that's very true." Gladwell expressed back.

"The early bird catches the worm, hey Gladwell." Bog said while elbowing him several times.

"Yes, I suppose it does."

At that point Lady Betsy gathered all the guests around in the main drawing room and raised her glass of champagne.

"I'd like to thank everyone for attending tonight's event. It was a truly fantastic evening. Would anyone like to say something at this point?"

Bog cleared his throat and approached the podium which was really a guest dressed up as a steamer trunk that had been thrown overboard.

"Good evening ladies and gentlemen. Let me begin by saying that the grass is always greener on the other side."

"Here, here!" yelled a man dressed as small barnacle."

"Thank you. I'd also just like to add that beggars cannot be choosers. That an apple a day keeps the doctor away. And finally in closing, a watched pot never boils.

Chapter Apeteen
The International Bog Show

Bog was excited that he was going to be a contestant in the annual International Bog Show at Madison Square Kennel Club Arena Place. This was his first time in the competition and he was really looking forward to it. Doy had been training him on his positions, his trot and his speech to entertain. He finally felt ready.

On the day of the show they had breakfast at McDonald's. Doy had the Egg McChicken and Bog had a saucer of milk. He didn't want a heavy meal before the show. When they arrived at the Madison Square Kennel Club Arena Place, Bog became a little intimidated. There was Scotty Bog who had won the last three competitions. This bog had swagger. He had a nice kilt, a killer Scottish accent and was able to throw the caber half a mile. A mile if it was a clear day. To say Bog was intimidated would be to say it twice as it was already said in the fourth sentence of this paragraph.

Some of the other contestants were Bella the Beagle, Sherman the Charpee, Felipe the Poodle and Fred the Irish Wolf hound and Franz the Zebra. Franz had escaped from the New York City

Zoo but no one could convince him he wasn't a bog.

As the show began, bright lights were flicked on to illuminate the great arena. From the locker room came the three judges; Patty O'Malley, Freddie Cheddarton and Sir Stanley Boatswain.

"Good afternoon ladies and gentlemen and welcome to the 104th International Bog Show. Please hold all of your applause until this evening when you go to bed. And now, our first event is the Incessant Trot. And our first competitor is Scotty Bog!"

Scotty Bog ran onto the floor and began to trot like no one's business. (Of course there is no such business as the Incessant Trot but get my…my…is it drip? Yes that's it. You get my drip). Anyway, Scotty Bog was on fire…literally. He had ran so hard on the carpet that he had caused friction and ignited his kilt. He had to put out with a fire extinguisher. Scotty was in no condition to continue the show because he was dead.

"Next we have…Bog. Just plain Bog"

Bog started off well, he went several feet without incident. His fifth step though caused him to trip on the carpet and fell flat on his face. Doy quickly retrieved him and he was soon on his way again. After another ten feet was down on the ground again. This time he was in such agony that he began to howl and roll around the carpet looking for treats. Doy ran over to him and kicked him hard in the foot which brought him around. As Bog rose to his feet, he trembled and then fell over again. Doy knelt down and tried to encourage him by punching him on the nose. Doy whispered in his ear how great it would be if he could finish the trot. He reminded Bog that since the 17th century everyone in his family had been able to trot. They could trot on a cliff's ledge, they could trot on a precarious slope, they could trot on top of a mountain, they could trot with one foot tied behind their backs. “Bog, it's in your blood buddy. Now go get ‘em!” Bog sat up and then looked Doy in the eye. He nodded his head and got back up. Bog decided at that point that he needed to make up some points because of his lack of trotting skills. He produced a jetpack from his backpack he was wearing and began to shoot around the great arena. People were impressed with his flying skills and he soon had a standing ovation before flying directly into a pillar. Doy soon revived Bog and took him back to the sidelines. The judges convened and Bog was awarded three and half points.

All the other contestants scored at least 150 points each on their trots so Bog was way behind. The next event was the “Fetch.” All the other contestants did well as their masters threw sticks and they were able to retrieve them with no problem. Doy however used a drain pipe from their house as a stick because he apparently couldn't locate any "sticks," he said using his fingers to make air quotes. The drain pipe was heavy and Bog could not grasp it with his teeth so he was awarded zero points. He then placed the drain pipe on top of Doy's head. He was then award 10 points for the humorous use of drain pipes.

Now Bog's only hope was to score well on the speech to entertain. He had been practicing the speech all day and night and felt confident he would win that event.

"And now Bog will entertain you with a speech…"

Bog, now wearing an expensive Armani tuxedo approached the podium.

"Good afternoon ladies and gentlemen. Distinguished guests and our esteemed judges. It was once said by Sir Thomas More that you can never go home again. Well, any bog will tell you that's true. But the truth is, we can all go home again. In fact, Doy, it's almost 4 p.m. which is time for my feeding. Let's go!"

And with that the audience exploded with applause. Some of them actually exploded but the ones that didn't explode kept applauding while a cleaning crew cleaned-up the people that had exploded. It was an afternoon to remember and Bog had won the day. To celebrate Doy and Bog went home and baked a frozen pizza. While we use the term “baked” loosely, the boys were eventually able to consume it. What a day it had been.

CHAPTER Somin' Somin'
Just Sayin'

Doy and Bog were getting ready for their speech writing class when they decided they needed to come up with some new sayings. They began to ponder the origins of other sayings from long ago…

- *Killing two stones with one bird*
- *Costs you an alarm and an egg*
- *Can't budge a cook by its lover*
- *A tenny for your pots*
- *Pinkled tink*
- *Leave no turn unstoned*
- *Let the bat out of the cab*

CHAPTER Twenpy

Doy and Bog form a Rap Group

Doy and Bog decided they wanted to form a rap group. They had been inspired by Snoop Bog, 2 Chainz-link Fence, M&M (Who wears a candy (w)rapper), 50 Sense and MicroHard's Gil Bates.

They started DJing at a local club next to their dwelling called Starbucks. Since it was a coffee shop they were soon turned away and decided to work on their sound in their garage. Doy had a cool synthesizer and Bog had an even cooler banjo with one string. They created some interesting sounds and recorded them on their recording thingy. They spent hours mixing their tapes and sauces and soon had their recipe of sound!

The first night of the Chinchilla festival in Taos, New Mexico City was exciting. Although not invited, the boys took to the stage right after Nancy Sinatra's performance of These Boots were Made for Walking. Like a couple of crazed, out-of-control electronica nerds, the boys began to play their tapes and then dance around the stage. Doy took the mike and began to rap (sung to the medley of "boom-te-boom, boom-te-boom"…

You take your gift
You take some paper
You take some ribbon
You take some Scotch tape
You make a package
And that's a Christmas Wrap

When the boys tried to do a second verse, everyone in the audience stormed the stage and set fire to their recording thingy.

While the boys had not really understood the difference between "rap" and "wrap," their song was still popular in other places. It reached number #412 in Iceland (The Icelandic Music Chart system only has 20 places but the lady that runs it says that #412 is where she thinks the song would land if it could go up that high. She was later indicted for embezzlement in an elaborate scheme whereby she sold forged Stan Musial ((by the way this is the second reference to Stan Musial in this book – see page blah blah blah)) baseball cards that were really just drawings her 8 year son made with crayon, as well as tapering with recording thingys) and number #8 in New Guinea.

Where they really made impact was in Mongolia. Their (w)rap song made it to #1 in Outer Mongolia and #2 in Inner Mongolia.

Blekki-Bie-
Saldarnulabukfromtingotobedforthelasttimeother

wiseIwillcallyourfather (Loosely translated as Bill Smith from Mongolian to English) wrote in the Outer Mongolian Evening Gazzette…

I've never heard sounds like this before. I wish I could shoot myself. Luckily I only grazed the side of my face and the bullet ripped off my ear. Now I never have to listen to music ever again!!!

Fifi Babblingbrookhocuspocus (Loosely translated as Bill Smith from Mongolian to Albanian and then to English) wrote in the Inner Mongolian Free Press…

I like their sound. Normally combining a synthesizer with a one-string banjo doesn't do it for me, but this duo somehow manages to make it work. I would like to buy them a coffee!!! I can only afford one though. One them will have to buy their own coffee. What do I look like Stan Musial?

The duo eventually broke up and started solo careers. Doy became a highly successful Japanese Kota player and Bog was eventually able to buy more banjo strings.

CHAPTER Twenty-Won
Micronezia

One day, the boys decided that they wanted to see things at a micro-level where they could interact with "small stuff like molecules."

"Doy, how are we going to get small enough to look at micro-stuff?"

"I'm not sure but I was watching Alice in Waunderland the other day…"

"Waunderland? You mean Wonderland?"

"No, Waunderland. You know, the story by Carrol Lewis?"

"Don't you mean Lewis Carrol?"

"No. Different guy. Anyway, in the story Alice takes some food and it makes her shrink. I wonder if we can get a hold of the same thing that will make us shrink?"

"We could try. But why don't we just use my shrinking potion I just created?"

"Shrinking potion?"

"Yes, look." Bog shows Doy a bottle of soda.

"Isn't that just a bottle of soda?" Doy asked.

"Yes, but my mother said that if I keep drinking soda it will stunt my growth."

"Really, but we would probably have to drink a lot of it?"

"Yes, I have over fifty bottles in the garage."

"Well, let's get to work."

After several days of drinking nothing but soda, the boys ended up in the hospital. After being discharged from the hospital they continued to drink the soda. Eventually it began to work. They could feel themselves shrinking. Actually there was so much sugar in their system they began to hallucinate.

"Doy, since we have shrunk sufficiently, let's go fill the bathtub with water and then use our toy submarine to look at micro-stuff."

"That's a great idea Bog. Let's get our trunks on."

After the boys got their trunks on and filled the bathtub with water, they entered their toy submarine. They launch their submersible from "Port Farts" which was the soap dish. Descending through the suds they eventually landed on the bottom of the tub. They took out their scuba gear and entered the water. By then they had shrunk to microscopic levels.

"Wow Bog, this place is incredible. It's like swimming through a petri-dish."

"I know Doy, it's incredible."

"Look, who is that really attractive girl over there?"

"I'm not sure, let's ask her."

"Hello. My name is Doy and this is Bog."

"Hello boys, my name is Molly Cule. You can call me Molly."

"Wow, it's great to meet you Molly. How long have you lived here?"

"Oh, about 13 billion years. Where are you from?"

"We are from the surface world."

"Oh, is that like Akron?"

"Yep, very much like Akron."

"That's swell. I'd like you to meet some of my friends. Over here is Sal, Sal Monella."

"Hi Sal!"

"Hi boys!"

"Over here we have Vi, Vi Rus."

"Good to meet you boys," Vi Rus said, batting her eyelashes and speaking with a coy sexy voice.

"And this little guy over here is Adam."

"Hi Adam. What are those things circling around you?"

"Oh those are neutrons, electrons and protons."

"Isn't that kind of annoying?"

"Not really. They help me keep my balance."

"Now, if you boys have time, we can take you to a little party we are having. Would you like that?" Molly asked.

"Sure, we have all the time in the world."

"Great, we are just going to this corner of the bathtub over here."

When they arrived there was what appeared to be a nightclub with pulsating lights and a driving beat.

"Wow, what is this place," Doy asked.

"It's the Petri-disco, Let's dance.

For the next several hours the boys danced with their new friends. When they tired, Vi Rus asked them if they would like to go to her place. Molly took the boys aside.

"I wouldn't go there boys, she might infect you."

The boys agreed and told Vi that they needed to get back home.

"I'm sorry to hear that boys. We could have had a really nice time. Most people find that I really get under their skin and that they can't keep me out of their lives they like me so much."

As Vi moved closer, the boys got scared and then swam as fast as they could in the other direction.

"Boys, it's just a dream. All you need to do is rub your shoes together and say, 'there's no place like Akron, there's no place like Akron.'"

The boys did as they were did as Molly instructed and soon they were in downtown Akron.

The boys looked around and were horrified by what they saw.

"So this is Akron. We don't even live in Akron!" Bog yelled.

CHAPTER Twenty-Too

Dating

The boys were asked out on a play date by their neighbors Cirl and Gat. Doy had always liked Cirl and Bog tolerated Gat. They decided to double-date and go to the movies. Doy bought Cirl a cornpop with dosa and Bog bought Gat a box of Senior Mints. The movie was Titanic 23 with Delindardo Capra and Jill Smith (the great, great, great, great, great granddaughter of Captain Smith who played the role of Captain Smith in the first movie).

The couples enjoyed the movie and afterward went for some creamice to discuss.

"I really like the ending on how the aliens saved everyone on the Titanic with their spaceship."

"It's a little hard to believe though. I mean it's a pretty well established fact that the Titanic sank with considerable loss of life."

"Cirl, you're a real buzzkill."

"I know but facts are facts and adding this very implausible ending is highly lugubrious."

"Lugubrious. You mean it's covered in gravy?" Bog said.

Immediately it was quiet and the sound of chickens chirping could be heard by a woman in downtown Prague.

"Wow, that woman has really good hearing."

"No silly, lugubrious means that they didn't have any of their lugs repaired," Doy said.

Immediately there was a molecule of ice thawed on the planet Nuplotonion.

"You are the silliest boys in the universe. Lugubrious means that it's silly to believe that people from the Titanic could be rescued by aliens from another galaxy.

"Oh, I see. That makes sense."

Later when the boys drove the girls to their house and parked outside.

"Well, I had a really nice time tonight Doy," Cirl said with a bright smile on her face. She began to pucker her lips and waited for Doy to kiss her.

"What in the world are you doing?"

"I'm waiting for you to kiss me."

"Well I am afraid that would be highly hydroponic of me if I presumed to offer such an act of propensity. You see I come from a long line of people who believe that segues are loquatious and redundant. Do you understand?

"Completely. Let's just keep things simple. Anyway it's time for me to get out of my Freudian slip and into some pajamas. Good night."

"Bog, I had an enjoyable evening," said Gat.

"Ditto."

Before the girls left, Cirl got her "gat."

"Okay boys, give me all of your money. I've got a Gat and I'm going to bust a cap into your assess if you don't give us what we want."

"Wait, wait, wait!" Doy interjected. "I thought "Gat" was just a interpolation of "Cat? I mean, your girlfriend is an actual girl and not a firearm correct?"

"Ah, you caught me. I just wanted to see if you fell for it."

With that the two couples burst into uncontrolled hysteria. They never saw each other ever again.

CHAPTER Twenty-Threep

Wild Life

Doy and Bog were flutterby hunting when they came across a giant rarebit.

"Wow, you are very large for a rarebit."

"I know. My mom says it's hormones."

"It must make it very difficult for you to go down the average rarebit hole?"

"Oh, yes. It requires that I get a jack hammer to create a large enough hole for me to go down."

"What do your parents say about it?"

"Oh, they've been very accommodating. Especially since I am able to bring home a lot of carrots."

"Okay bye!"

"Bye!"

The boys began to walk off toward their home, just beyond the camera angle.

"Don't you think we should help him Doy?" asked Bog.

"I don't think so."

"Why?"

"Well you know what they say. 'Don't go down that rarebit hole."

"Who says that?"

"You know… 'they.'"

“But who are ‘they’?”

“Who’s on first.”

“Who’s on first?”

“ ‘they.’”

“ ‘they’ who?”

“Wait, wait, wait! Let’s start all over. Who’s on first?”

“Joe DiMaggio.”

“Who’s on second?”

“John Lennon.”

“Who’s on third?”

“Peter Parker.”

“What are you doing?”

“I thought we were doing the Abbot and Costello thing?”

“Yeah, but why John Lennon and Peter Parker?”

“Just using a little creativity.”

“Yes, but then the bit doesn’t work.”

“Oh okay.”

“Now what?”

“I’m not sure. The author is running out of ideas.”

“Who’s the author?”

“A.M. Overett.”

“Boy, isn’t this a little egotistical to have the author including in this dialogue. I mean, what do we know about him?”

"Not sure, but he's been writing our words that we have been using throughout his book."

"What book?"

"The book we are in."

"Who's on first?"

And with that the author tore up the paper* he was writing on, rolled it into a little ball and threw it into the trash.

Several minutes later, the boys regained consciousness…

"Wow, Bog, where are we?"

"I don't know, but my head sure hurts."

"It looks like some sort of metal cirlindrical box."

"Yeah, and what are all these papers?"

"Looks like it's all of the authors bad ideas and mistakes."

"There sure are a lot of them."

"I know. The guy must be totally lame."

"What's this giant yellow thing?"

"Looks like a banana peel."

"And what's that thing?"

"Looks like a half-eaten sandwich."

"The guy is lame and a slob."

"Typical author I guess."

"Anyway, how do we get out of here?"

"Well, if we are just saying the words that the author is giving us, maybe we can give him words?"

"Okay, like what?"
"Hey author, get us outta of here!!!"
"I don't think it worked."
"Author, get us out of here!!!"

And so eventually the author allowed the boys to get out of the trashcan and they lived ever after.

**Word document on laptop*

www.ingramcontent.com/pod-product-compliance
Lightning Source LLC
Chambersburg PA
CBHW070839020826
48982CB00022B/1529/J
* 9 7 8 1 6 4 3 7 3 3 6 4 7 *